This book belongs to:

. . . .

For Jasper – J.W.

For Max McGinty – A.R.

This paperback edition published in 2011 by Andersen Press Ltd.
Published in Australia by Random House Australia Pty.,
Level 3, 100 Pacific Highway, North Sydney, NSW 2060.
First published in Great Britain in 2011 by Andersen Press Ltd.
Text copyright © Jeanne Willis, 2011
Illustration copyright © Adrian Reynolds, 2011
The rights of Jeanne Willis and Adrian Reynolds to be identified as the author and
illustrator of this work have been asserted by them in accordance with the
Copyright, Designs and Patents Act, 1988. All rights reserved.
Colour separated in Switzerland by Photolitho AG, Zürich. Printed and bound in Singapore.
Adrian Reynolds has used watercolour in this book.

10   9   8   7   6   5   4   3   2

British Library Cataloguing in Publication Data available. ISBN 978 1 84939 030 9

I'M SURE I SAW A DINOSAUR

Jeanne Willis

Adrian Reynolds

ANDERSEN PRESS

One foggy, groggy morning
By the salty, splashy sea . . .

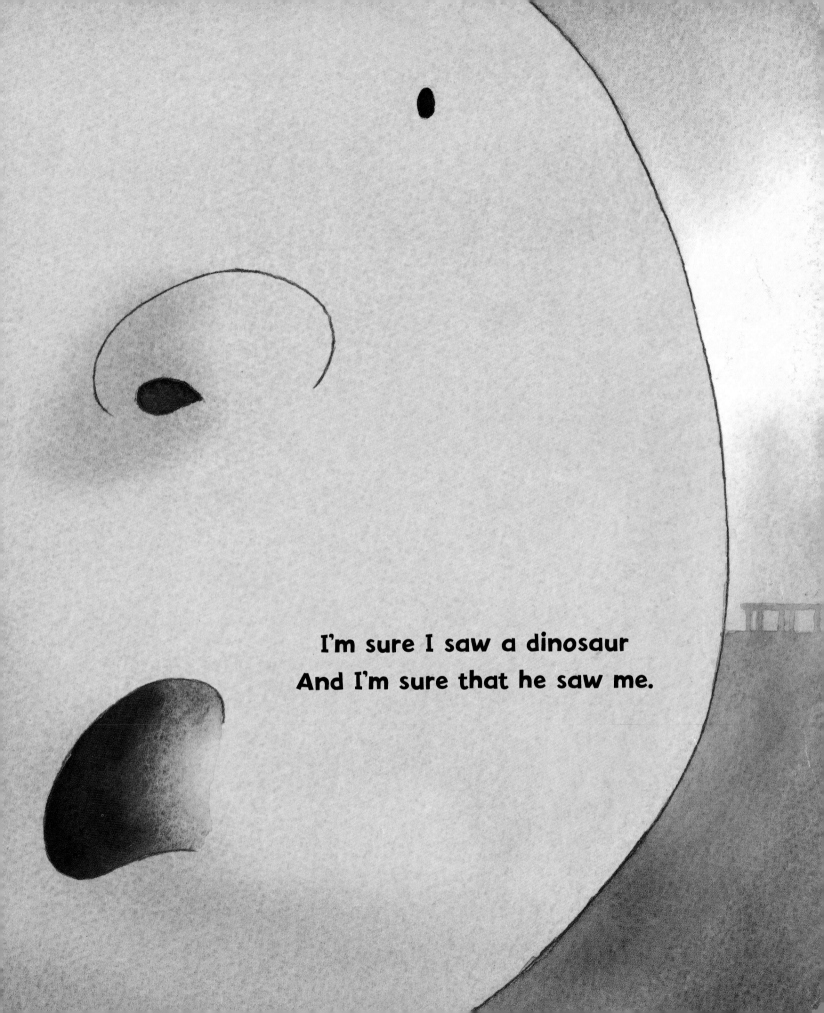

I'm sure I saw a dinosaur
And I'm sure that he saw me.

I ran and told the fisherman,

Who ran and told his mum,

Who ran and told the butcher
He must hurry up and come.

The butcher told the baker
And the baker told the vet
And they ran down to
the seashore
With a camera and a net.

"What's the matter?"
asked the priest.
"Now what is all the fuss?"
"A dinosaur's been seen!"
they said,
"We're sure it can see us!"

The priest told all the people
And each person told a friend;
They all came running down the beach
To Sandy Bottom End.

All the aunts and uncles came;
The nephews and the nieces.
All the grans and grandads came
In woolly hats and fleeces.

They came with sweets and sandwiches
And soup inside a flask,
Some didn't know why they were there
But didn't like to ask.

The newsmen came, the navy came
The captain called his crew,
"A dinosaur's been seen!" he said
"Make sure it can't see you!"

They came with ropes and motorboats
With cannons and with snares
They came with swords and submarines
And scientists and prayers.

The airforce came. The army came
And formed a human chain.
Men in parachutes arrived
And jumped out of a plane.

They came with dogs and divers
And binoculars and bait
And searched the sea for dinosaurs
From morning until late.

They sat out in the wind and snow
They sat out in the rain,
And none of them showed any sign
Of going home again.

They set up camp upon the sand
In tents and trucks and cars,
And still they sit and watch and wait
Beneath the moon and stars.

But will they see a dinosaur?
Or was my master plan . . .
To help my daddy sell ice creams?
He is the ice cream man!

No one comes to buy them
In the winter when it's cold.
Now everybody wants one;
Every cornet has been sold.

I'm sure I saw a dinosaur
But is it really true?
Come and buy an ice cream . . .

And perhaps you'll see one too!

Also by Jeanne Willis and Adrian Reynolds

9781842706282

9781842706985

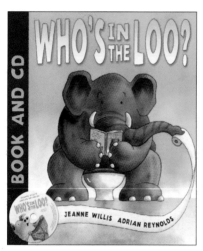

9781849390217

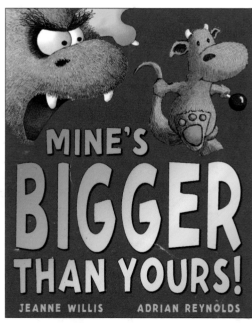

9781842708637

9781842709863